Thomas Stewart Denison

Under the Laurels

Thomas Stewart Denison

Under the Laurels

ISBN/EAN: 9783337335175

Printed in Europe, USA, Canada, Australia, Japan

Cover: Foto ©Andreas Hilbeck / pixelio.de

More available books at **www.hansebooks.com**

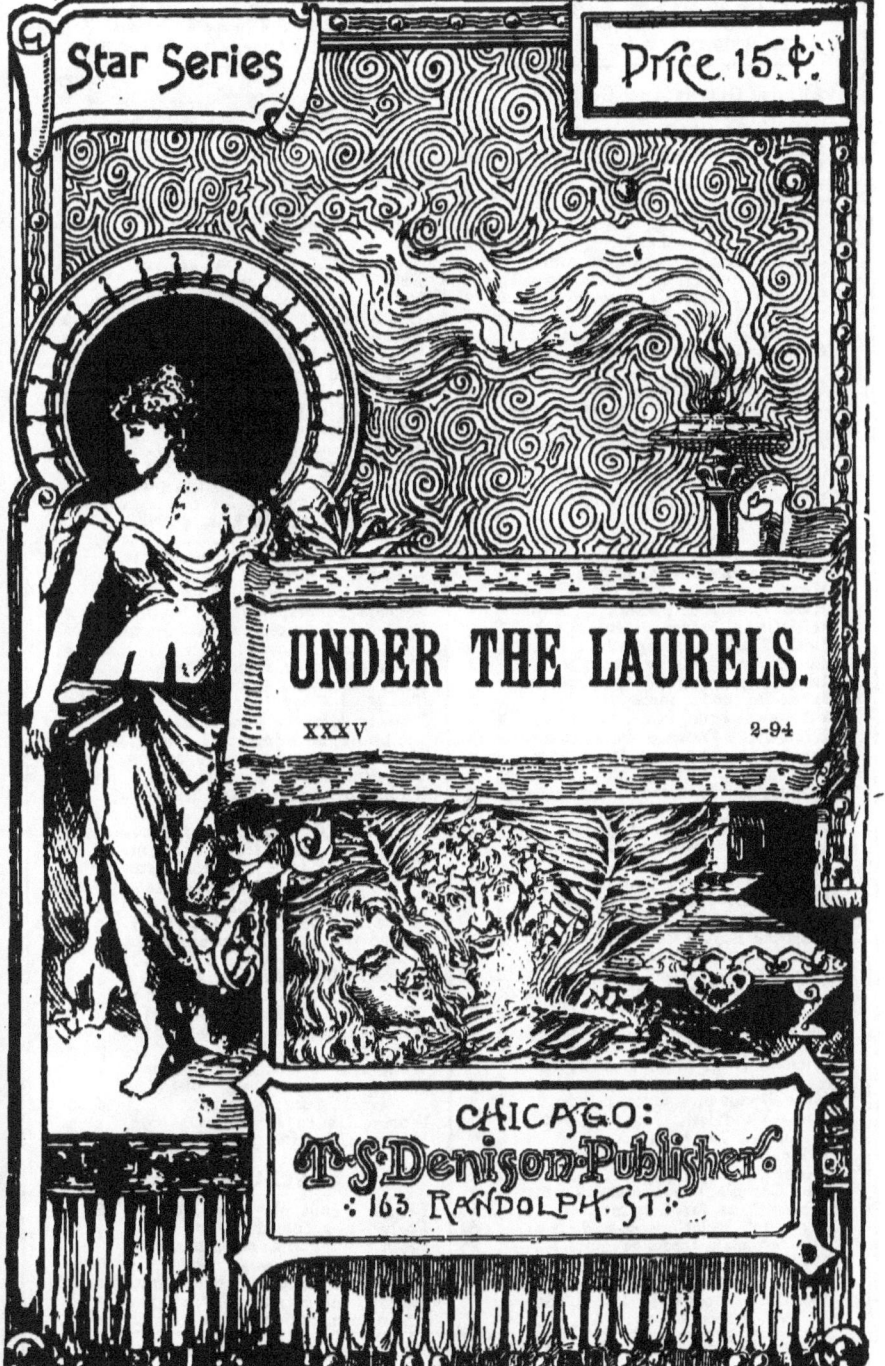

Star Series

Price. 15 ¢.

UNDER THE LAURELS.

XXXV

2-94

CHICAGO:
T. S. Denison Publisher.
163 RANDOLPH ST.

DENISON'S ACTING PLAYS.

ALTA SERIES, Price 25 Cents Each, Postpaid.   All Others 15 Cents Each.

	M.	F.
All that Glitters is not Gold, comedy, 2 acts, 2 hrs.	6	3
A Very Pleasant Ev farce, 30 m.	3	0
Assessor, sketch, 10 min.	3	2
Babes in Wood, burlesque, 25 m.	4	3
Borrowing Trouble, farce, 20 min.	3	5
Bad Job, farce, 30 min.	3	2
Bumble's Courtship, sketch, 18 m.	1	1
Bardell vs. Pickwick, farce, 25 m.	6	2
Christmas Ship, musical, 20 min.	4	3
Caste, comedy, 3 acts, 2 hrs. 30 m.	5	3
Cow that Kicked Chicago, 20 m.	3	2
Country Justice, farce, 15 min.	8	0
Circumlocution Office, 20 min.	6	0
Chimney Corner, drama, 2 acts, 1 hr., 30 min.	5	2
Cut off with a Shilling, farce, 25 m	2	1
Danger Signal, drama, 2 acts, 2 hrs.	7	4
Desperate Situation, farce, 25 min.	2	3
East Lynne, drama, 5 acts, 2 hrs.	8	7
Fair Encounter, 20 min	0	2
Family Strike, farce, 20 min.	3	3
Fruits of Wine Cup, temperance drama, 3 acts, 1 hr.	6	4
Friendly Move, sketch, 20 min.	5	0
Home, comedy, 3 acts, 2 hrs.	4	3
Homœopathy, farce, 30 min.	5	3
Hans Von Smash, farce, 30 min.	4	3
Hard Cider, temperance, 15 min.	4	2
Initiating a Granger, farce, 25 min.	8	0
In the Dark, farce, 25 min.	4	2
In the Wrong House, farce, 20 m.	4	2
Irish Linen Peddler, farce, 40 min.	3	3
Is the Editor In, farce, 20 min.	4	2
I'll Stay Awhile, farce, 20 min.	4	0
Ici on Parle Francais, farce, 40 m.	4	3
I'm not Mesilf at All, farce, 25 m.	3	2
John Smith, farce, 30 min.	5	3
Just my Luck, farce, 20 min.	4	3
Kansas Immigrants, farce, 20 m.	5	1
Kiss in the Dark, farce, 30 m.	2	3
Louva the Pauper, drama, 5 acts, 1 hr. 45 min.	9	4
Love and Rain, 20 min.	1	1
Larkins' Love Letters, farce, 50 m.	3	2
Lady of Lyons, 5 acts, 2 hrs. 30 m.	8	4
Limerick Boy, farce, 30 min.	5	2
Lost in London, drama, 3 acts, 1 h. 45 min.	6	3
London Assurance, comedy, 5 acts, 2 hrs. 30 min.	9	3
Lucky Sixpence, farce, 30 min.	4	2
Lucy's Old Man, sketch, 15 min.	2	3
Michael Erle, drama, 2 acts, 1 hr. 30 min.	8	3
Mike Donovan, a farce, 15 min.	1	3
Mitsu-Yu Nissi, Japanese Wedding, 1 hr. 15 min.	6	6
Model of a Wife, farce, 25 min.	3	2
Movement Cure, farce, 15 min.	5	0
Mrs Gamp's Tea, sketch, 15 min.	0	2
Misses Beers, farce, 25 min.	3	3
My Wife's Relations, comedy, 1 hr	4	6
My Jeremiah, farce, 20 min.	3	2
My Turn Next, farce, 50 min.	4	3
My Neighbor's Wife, farce, 45 min	3	3
Not Such a Fool as He Looks, comedy, 3 acts, 2 hrs.	5	3

	M.	F.
On Guard, farce, 25 min.	4	2
Only Daughter, drama, 3 acts, 1 hr. 15 min.	5	2
Our Country, drama, 3 acts, 1 hr.	10	3
Odds with Enemy, 5 acts, 2 hrs.	7	4
On the Brink, temperance drama, 2 acts, 2 hrs.	12	3
Out in the Streets, 1 h. 15 min.	6	4
Pet of Parsons' Ranch, frontier drama, 5 acts, 2 hrs.	9	3
Pets of Society, farce, 30 min.	0	7
Pull Back, farce, 20 min.	0	6
Pocahontas, musical burlesque, 1 hr	10	2
Parlor Entertainment, 25 min.	2	5
Played and Lost, sketch, 15 min.	3	2
Persecuted Dutchman, 35 min.	6	3
Quiet Family, farce, 45 min.	4	4
Regular Fix, farce, 50 min.	3	4
Rough Diamond, farce, 40 min.	4	3
Silent Woman, farce, 25 min.	2	1
Solon Shingle, comedy, 1 hr. 30 m.	7	2
Soldier of Fortune, comedy, 5 acts, 2 hrs. 20 min.	8	3
Seth Greenback, drama, 4 acts, 1 hr. 15 min.	7	3
Schoolma'am (The), drama, 4 acts, 1 hr. 45 min.	6	5
Slasher and Crasher, 1 hr. 15 min.	5	2
Squeers' School, sketch, 18 min.	4	2
Sparkling Cup, temperance drama 5 acts, 2 hrs.	12	4
Taming a Tiger, farce, 20 min.	3	0
That Rascal Pat, farce, 35 min.	3	2
Too Much Good Thing, 50 min.	3	6
Twenty Minutes Under an Umbrella, 20 min.	1	1
Two Gents in a Fix, farce, 20 min.	2	0
Two Puddifoots, farce, 40 min.	3	3
Ticket of Leave Man, drama, 4 acts, 2 hrs. 45 min.	8	3
Turn Him Out, farce, 50 min.	3	3
Toodles, drama, 2 acts, 1 hr. 15 m.	6	2
Ten Nights in a Barroom, temperance drama, 5 acts, 2 hrs.	11	5
Two Ghosts in White, sketch. 25 m	0	8
Uncle Dick's Mistake, farce, 20 m.	3	2
Under the Laurels, drama, 5 acts, 1 hr. 45 min.	5	4
Wanted a Correspondent, farce, 1 h	4	4
Wide Enough for Two, farce, 50 m	5	2
Which Will He Marry farce, 30 m	2	8
Won at Last, comedy, 3 acts, 1 hr. 45 m	7	3
Wonderful Letter, farce, 25 min.	4	1
Women of Lowenburg, historical sketch, 5 scenes, 50 min.	10	10
Wooing Under Difficulties, 35 min.	4	3
Yankee Detective, 3 acts, 2 hrs	8	3

ALTA SERIES—25c. each.

	M.	F.
Beggar Venus, play, 2 hrs. 30 min.	6	4
Early Vows, comedy, 1 hr	4	2
From Sumter to Appomattox, military play, 2 hrs. 30 min.	6	2
Shadow Castle, play, 2 hrs. 30 min.	5	4
Jedediah Judkins, comedy, 2 h. 30 m.	7	5
Uncle Josh, comedy, 2 hrs	8	3

T. S. DENISON, Publisher, 163 Randolph St., Chicago.

Under the Laurels

A Drama In Five Acts,

By T. S. DENISON,

AUTHOR OF

Odds with the Enemy; Initiating a Granger; Wanted, A Correspondent; A Family Strike; Seth Greenback; Hans Von Smash; Borrowing Trouble; Two Ghosts in White; The Pull-Back; Country Justice; The Assessor; The Sparkling Cup; Louva the Pauper; Our Country; The School-Ma'am; The Kansas Immigrants; The Irish Linen Peddler; Is the Editor In? An Only Daughter; Pets of Society: Too Much of a Good Thing; Hard Cider, Etc.

———

CHICAGO:

T. S. DENISON.

CHARACTERS.

MRS. MILFORD,
ROSE MILFORD.
POLLY DOWLER.
SOOKY BUTTON.
KYLE ("Ky.") BRANTFORD.

FRANK COLEWOOD
IKE HOPPER.
BOB BUTTON.
ZEKE.
SHERIFF.

COSTUMES—Modern.

STAGE DIRECTIONS.

R means *right* as the actor faces the audience; L, *left*, C, *center*, etc.

NOTE—Lightning may be produced by blowing finely powdered rosin into a candle flame. Thunder by rattling a large piece of sheet iron. Rain by allowing beans to fall through a long narrow box studded on the bottom with pegs or with oblique partitions leaving a narrow opening on opposite sides alternately. Moonlight may be produced by the strong white light of a burning tableau powder.

SYNOPSIS.

ACT I.

The Milford Estate. The Contested Will. Conspiracy of Brantford and Mrs. Milford.

ACT II.

The will set aside. Frank and Rose penniless. Brantford's annoying attentions to Rose. Quarrel of Frank and Brantford. The latter plots vengeance. Bob Button, the spy. Rose's humiliating situation as a menial.

ACT III.

Meeting of the Regulators at the haunted cabin. Ike and Zeke concealed to listen. Their great danger. SCENE II.—Cliffville jail. Frank under arrest. Assailed by Bob Button. Desperate encounter. Frank escapes, and soon Rose enters to release him. Button's triumph cut short by the timely arrival of Ike and Zeke. Storm scene. The flight.

ACT IV.

Brantford's absolute power over the Milford family. His continued attentions to Rose. His threats to foreclose the mortgage.

ACT V.

Attempted escape of Rose. Her re-capture. Brantford's triumph suddenly ended by a sheriff's posse. Happy denouement.

UNDER THE LAURELS.

ACT I.

SCENE.—*Milford's parlor. A room elegantly furnished, indicating wealth and refinement. Window in flat C. A handsome center table by window. Chairs on either side of table, and R. and L. vases, books, etc. Seated MRS. MILFORD and ROSE in conversation as the curtain rises.*

Mrs. M. Rose, has Mr. Brantford arrived yet?

Rose. I think not, mother. He was not in sight down the road a moment ago. I told Zeke to show him in at once when he came.

Mrs M. That was right, Rose. I am anxious to see him. These business affairs are very perplexing, and Mr. Brantford is such a help to us.

R. I do not like him, mother. I think it would be prudent to watch him a little.

Mrs. M. Rose, I am grieved to see that you are suspicious. Mr. Brantford has helped me greatly to arrange our affairs since my husband's death. His sympathy and kindness have been doubly grateful to me since things have not turned out as I hoped they would, Rose.

R. Mother, I am very sorry you are dissatisfied with the terms of father's will. A small portion would have satisfied me. But it is all yours, mother, while you live.

Mrs. M. It would have been more fitting if the will had so stated it. Mr. Milford must surely have been laboring under a strange delusion, to leave the bulk of his property to you who were not his child, while his wife got only a third, and another heir nothing. Remember, Rose, you were only an orphan who found a home with my husband's family. Why should you claim so large a portion of his fortune? Frank Colewood's right is just as good as yours.

R. (*Brushing away a tear.*) Mother, I know I was only a friendless orphan, but Mr. Milford was a kind father to me, and his wife was a gentle mother. They had no children, but I did not ask their wealth. I would willingly divide with Frank, but I cannot bear to hear father accused of unfairness. He was too good. Frank never came to live with us till a year or two before you came.

Mrs. M. Child, I accuse no one. Doubtless your father's untimely death prevented his latest wishes from being carried into effect.

R. Mother, there is enough for all. Why should we disagree about it? I would willingly give up all to you were it possible. There is much yet to be arranged before the estate is finally settled.

Mrs. M. Mr. Brantford is rendering important aid.

R. Has he paid over all the money he has collected?

Mrs. M. No; he has collected sufficient to settle his own claims against the estate. You know that he and Mr. Milford entered into a partnership in the cattle business, and that Brantford advanced most of the money. That must be repaid.

R. I don't believe that Ky. Brantford advanced the money. I think he is a dishonest man.

Mrs. M. Rose, you are too young to express such decided opinions, especially on subjects which you do not understand. (*Exit Mrs. M., R.*)

R. I know when I like people and when I don't, and I don't like Kyle Brantford, that's sure. Father hinted to me more than once that Brantford was not above suspicion. It is a shame to squabble over dead people's property! I hate it!

Enter FRANK *L.*

Frank. What is that you hate so energetically, Rose?

R. Oh, nothing!

F. Can you as truthfully say, oh, nobody?

R. No, I can't! It's Ky. Brantford, if you must know, Frank.

F. Well, Rose, all I can say is I think he is a villain. Beware of Ky. Brantford!

R. Frank, I am worried nearly to death. If it wasn't for you I don't know what I should do.

F. Probably you could get along well enough without me, but I should miss the budding "Mountain Rose." You have been a true sister to me since I came here a friendless orphan eight years ago.

R. Oh, those happy years! I scarcely dare think of them. They recall so vividly the uncertainties of the present. Mother is very much dissatisfied of late with her portion.

F. She has evil counsel. Ky. Brantford is plotting mischief.

R. Others have more right to complain than she. (*A pause.*) Oh, Frank! why were you not mentioned in the will?

F. The reason is plain, Rose—or perhaps it would be best now to say Miss Milford—Mr. Milford loved you dearly as his own child.

R. And so he loved you. Frank, your formality pains me. It is out of place between us.

F. Yes, Rose, if we were to continue as brother and sister, but the time has come when we can no longer continue our past relations. I am only the poor boy still, while you are the daughter and the heiress.

R. Frank, your manner is unkind.

F. (*Bitterly.*) It is so! My position in the world is yet to win. Yours is already won. If Mr. Milford had wished it otherwise he would have spoken. Perhaps it is better as it is after all.

R. Frank, I cannot bear to hear you speak so. Only wait till everything is settled, and you shall have your share.

F. Share! I claim no share. I worked for wages and I got them. I make no complaint. Waiting brings me nothing that I prize. 'Tis a short time at least till I must seek my fortune elsewhere, so I might as well go at once.

R. Frank, don't go. We need you. Please don't think of it. (*Coaxingly.*) Won't you stay?

F. Rose, it is hard to refuse.

R. You will not refuse your sister?

F. (*Turning away, aside.*) Sister! I hate that word. Shall I tell her all? (*To Rose.*) My decision has been reached. Why tarry?

Enter POLLY, *R, unobserved.*

R. (*Thoughtfully.*) If you must leave I wish you success wherever you go. I am grieved that you will not stay, but as soon as it can be arranged half of all I own shall be yours.

F. Thank you, Rose, thank you. Your offer is a generous one.

R. (*Eagerly.*) And you will stay?

F. No!

Polly. Frank Colewood, you are a dunce. (*Rose starts.*)

F. Thank you, Polly, for your opinion; unlike yourself, it is plain.

P. And why is it like Miss Rose?

F. I give it up.

P. Because it is *true.*

R. Don't flatter me, Polly.

F. Polly, you are brushing up your wits pretty lively.

P. Yes, and I'll brush them up till I've convinced you that you are a dunce for leaving a good home.

R. I wish you could convince him.

P. Miss Rose, if you will just step into the kitchen and watch my cake a few minutes, I'll see if I can't find that needle cushion I lost yesterday. I must have it.

R. Very good, Polly, I'll mind your cake, just five minutes, remember. (*Exit Rose, R.*)

F. Now, Polly, let us skirmish around after that needle cushion

P. Pshaw, Frank, I'm not going to look for any needle cushion. I reckon you'll not get mad if I tell you something.

F. Not unless it's something calculated to stir a fellow up pretty badly.

P. Oh, it is not bad at all. You see I have been about the house so long that I feel like one of the family.

F. Oh, don't spare my feelings. I'm only a hired man now.

P. But you might be more.

F. What do you mean?

P. I mean you are in love with Rose. Why don't you marry her instead of talking about leaving?

F. Polly, I shall never be a pensioner on any woman's bounty.

P. Frank Colewood, I told you you were a dunce.

F. I haven't denied it, Polly.

P. Then claim your own. Isn't the property as much yours as Rose's? Did not Mr. Milford always say so? She is an adopted daughter; you are an adopted son.

F. His *will* don't say so!

P. That will was made several years ago. Besides nobody seems to understand it.

F. I will abide by it, and I don't believe Mrs. Milford can break it.

P. I'm afraid they will do something that is not right. Mrs. Milford is a good enough sort of person as things go, but that Ky. Brantford is a—a—

F. Villain!

P. That's the word I wanted. Strange I couldn't think of it. He's too cute to be honest. Frank, do you love Rose?

F. I would die for her.

P. Nonsense, what would be the use of dyin' for her? Live for her, and don't talk of runnin' away when there is danger.

F. Running away? Is that what you call it? I thought you knew me better.

P. I didn't mean to offend you, Frank, but unless I miss my guess, there's goin' to be right smart o' trouble here. I've hearn things maybe you don't hear. That Bob Button is not the truest man in the world. Don't you tell him anything. This family needs friends.

F. Everybody needs them.

P. Yes, but *good* friends. Frank, it is your *duty* to stay.

F. Do you think so?

P. When Mr. Milford was thrown from his horse, and lay dying under the laurel bushes, with no one there but you and a stranger, did he not give you a charge?

F. Yes, his last words were, "Frank, take care of the family (*aside*), and marry Rose." (*Aloud.*) The family is able to take care of itself.

Enter BOB BUTTON, *L, unobserved.*

P. No, there is danger ahead. Don't go.
F. Well, I'll not go, Polly. I'll stay and see things in better shape. (*Sees Bob.*) Oh, are you here Button?
P. (*Quickly passing Frank to R.*) Oh, dear, he has heard me. (*Exit, R.*)
F. Button, what do you want?
B. I guess you had better lay off some more work. I'm done fixin' that wall.
F. Where is Zeke?
B. He is not back from the post-office.
F. It takes that nigger a long time to go to the post-office. Can you replace the barn door yourself, Bob?
B. I 'low not, Mr. Colewood.
F. Then I'll help you myself. (*Exit both, L.*)

Enter POLLY, *R.*

P. Thank goodness he didn't hear any more than he did. He's a regular spy. Now I must put this room to rights, Missus Milford says company's coming. (*Dusts furniture vigorously.*)

Enter IKE HOPPER, *R.*

Ike. How dye do, Polly? (*Stands holding his straw hat.*)
P. (*Hardly looking up.*) I'm well enough.
I. I reckon so, Polly. Been that way long?
P. Don't bother me Ike, I'm in a dreadful hurry to get this room put to rights. Why did you come right into this room?
I. I saw Rose Milford in the kitchen and she 'lowed I could see you if I came right in hyar. (*Pinches Polly's arm.*) Say, can I see you?
P. Yes, and hear me, too, if you don't behave. But what made you call at this time of day, Mr. Hopper?
I. *Mr. Hopper!* Gosh! that fairly takes my breath, Polly. Why, Jerusalem! you'll be callin' me 'Squire Hopper next. Polly, you an' me don't need to pile it on quite so thick as that.
P. (*Rather curtly.*) Speak for yourself, Isaac Hopper.
I. Now, Polly, don't get your dander up. I didn't mean anything.
P. I don't like to see people act silly.
I. Neither do I. Don't you tell anybody and I won't. Polly, that's a mighty nice dress you have on. (*Slips close beside her.*) That kaliker must a cost twelve and a half cents a yard. (*Feels*

I. Well, it looks pooty, but that's an awful waste of money.

P. Do you like it, Ike?

I. You're right I do. It's the nicest thing I've seen for a long time. (*Puts his arm around her.*) Polly, do you know what I came in from work just now for?

P. No! What did you come for?

I. (*Puzzled.*) I came for—for—what the deuce did I come for? Oh, I came to inquire about yer horse rake!

P. *My* horse rake?

I. No, I meant the *family* horse rake.

P. Then you had better go to the barn if you want the horse rake. (*Withdraws from him.*)

I. No, I meant the *horse radish.* (*Pronounce reddish.*) I knowed it was something found in the kitchen. Polly do you like horse radish?

P. Middlin' like. Do you?

I. (*Gets close to Polly again.*) Yes siree, I like everything that is good. (*Suddenly steals a kiss.*)

Enter ZEKE, *suddenly, R.*

P. (*Slaps Ike hard.*) How do you like that?

I. (*Sees Zeke.*) Miss Dowler, when you try to dig a hay seed out o' my eye, I wish you would be a little more keerful. (*Claps handkerchief to his eyes.*)

Zeke. Say, Massa Hopper, are you shore dat was a hay pod? Wasn't it a little piece of horse radish? Dat's mighty lively medicine to get into de eyes.

I. Why, is that you Zeke? I thought I heard the door open.

P. Did you get any letters for me, Zeke?

I. De train done left de track down de river, an' de mail was desput akerse to day, so I jes' went into de drug grocery an' got some medicine pamphlidges. Got one apiece, Miss Polly. Heah's you's. (*Hands one to Polly.*)

P. Git out with your almanix.

Z. Massa Hopper, have one? 'Spect it tells when to pull de horse radish.

I. Yes, I'll take one. (*Takes almanac, opens and reads.*) "Nigger invented, year one. First wool crop, same year.

Z. Dat's a berry good crop. Mighty sight surer nor cotton.

P. Do stop your nonsense, Zeke. Did you see anyone coming as you came in?

Z. Yes, seed Massa Brantford ride up to de front gate.

I. Plague his skin!

Z. What you gwine to plague his skin for?

I. Because it's good for nothing else.

P. You and Zeke must go at once. Mrs. Milford may come down any minit.

I. All right, then, here goes. Good bye, Polly. (*Throws a kiss. Zeke throws a kiss, unseen by Ike, with extravagant gestures, and Polly gives him a violent blow with the broom handle.*)

Z. Polly, I dropped sumfin'. Did you find it? (*Exit hastily L as Polly dives at him again.*)

P. Good gracious! I wish it was slavery times and I was that nigger's boss. He's the tormentenest thing! (*Bell heard.*) Just hear that bell! Brantford always rings it as if he owned the whole plantation. (*Exit Polly, L.*)

Enter POLLY, *L, showing in* KY. BRANTFORD.

Brantford. Polly, will you have the kindness to inform Mrs. Milford that I am waiting?

P. Yes, sir. (*Exit, L.*)

B. (*Pacing floor.*) All goes well; I could not wish it better. Milford's debtors are liberal and pay promptly and the estate is in no hurry to ask me to settle up. It's mighty lucky I have *influence* with the county court. If the young lady, the sweet Mountain Rose, is disposed to listen to my suit I will have the will approved and the property will be hers and mine. If not it shall be *mine*. I rather think the widow cares something for me, and it is just as well for the present that she does. Ha! its better to be born lucky than rich, that I can swear to, for my luck has never deserted me.

Enter MRS. MILFORD, *L*

Mrs. M. Good afternoon, Mr. Brantford, I am very glad to see you.

B. Good day, Mrs. Milford, I hope I have not kept you in suspense?

Mrs. M. Oh, no! but I expected you a little earlier. Have a seat. (*They take seats R and L of table.*)

B. We will proceed at once to business. I have little news for you. I am still endeavoring to collect some of those doubtful claims of your husband's. I am getting along fairly well, but people are dreadful slow pay nowadays. As you know, your husband's sudden death prevented the final settlement of our partnership in the cattle business. A very pretty sum was due me, and I am just paying myself, so to speak. I will render a statement of transactions any time you wish it.

Mrs. M. There is no need of hurry at all in the matter. You are a business man, and everything is safe in your hands.

B. Oh, perfectly safe, madam, still business is business, and it would be well for you to look a little after your own affairs.

Mrs. M. It is unnecessary when I have such excellent assistance always at hand.

B. You flatter me, Mrs. Milford, but I shall try to do the best I can.

Mrs. M. You were at Cliffville to-day I believe, Mr. Brantford. Did you learn anything new in regard to our will case?

B. Very little. The case which should have been disposed of months ago will soon come before the court. I think it safe to say, that under circumstances which may be fully shown in the testimony, the will is certain to be set aside.

Mrs. M. You mean that it may easily be proved that my husband never legally adopted Rose as his daughter?

B. Hum—yes, the testimony *may* show that.

Mrs. M. It *must* show it. Then if Rose is not an heir, neither is Frank, and the property is all mine.

B. Still, the children might reasonably expect *something*, but that could all be safely left to your generosity. No one doubts your sense of justice in this matter.

Mrs. M. I should of course make *some* provision for them. Frank Colewood would ask nothing and Rose could not expect to occupy the station she has usurped. I certainly do not consider her *my* daughter. However, she may stay if she wishes.

B. I should think a small sum in ready cash would induce Frank to go elsewhere and set up for himself.

Mrs. M. Would you advise me to let him go?

B. I certainly should advise it.

Mrs. M. I have always considered Frank an honest young man.

B. Doubtless he is honest. But remember, Mrs. Milford, he was a waif. You don't know his antecedents, and you can't tell what danger may lurk in his character. Blood will tell.

Mrs. M. True, I had not thought of that. I will hint the matter to him.

B. Never hint anything in business. Discharge him. By the way, how do you like that new man I sent you, Bob Button?

Mrs. M. Frank says he is a strong hand. That is all I know about him.

B. He is a good fellow. Keep him by all means. He can oversee the plantation when Frank leaves. That reminds me I wish to see Bob before I go.

Mrs. M. (*Rising.*) I will have him called.

B. No, don't take that trouble, I will see him as I leave.

Mrs. M. He is splitting kitchen wood, I think; it is no trouble to call him. (*Exit Mrs. M., R.*)

B. I must see the Mountain Rose before I go and settle matters at once. I have wealth, health and strength. All I need is a wife. The grass of many summers has grown over the grave of the first Mrs. Brantford, the wife of my boyhood. God bless her, she was a true loving wife, and I—(*stops short*) let that pass now. I can't expect much love for I am incapable of feeling any, but I will try to secure beauty. I fancy I am no bad figure yet, with my forty years. Beauty and money are trump cards in matrimony.

Enter Bob *R.*

Bob. Mrs. Milford said you wanted to see me, Ky.

B. Ky! Is that your style of address when you are in the company of ladies and gentlemen?

Bob. That's what they call you in some ·other company I know of, Ky. Brantford.

B. Hold your tongue! You are here to hear not to speak.

Bob. (*Doggedly.*) I reckon maybe the time'll come when you'll want me to talk.

B. Well, what have you to say?

Bob. (*With a sneer.*) I thought you'd change your tune before long.

B. Button, can't you learn civility?

Bob. I might from a civil master, Brantford. We've had right smart dealin's in our time. Some of 'em the less said about the better.

B. Then don't mention them! Don't I pay well? But I don't pay you to tell me what I know already.

Bob. I 'spose your pay is *good enough.* I reckon it might be a leetle *bigger.* But it ain't *that* I care for. We've learned down south hyar that when one man plays master somebody else must play slave. Brantford, I ain't a nigger, and I ain't exactly poor white trash, nuther.

B. All right, Bob. Let that go. I was only giving you a little advice. But I see you are not inclined to take it. Have you anything to report?

Bob. Nuthin' worth mentionin'.

B. Watch Frank Colewood and learn his plans. Get his confidence.

Bob. I ain't the man to get his confidence. He's poor but dev'lish proud. He wants to sort with fine folks.

B. Let him, if he can. Asa Milford isn't backing him now.

Bob. I heard this· mornin' that he wanted to leave and the women folks wouldn't let him.

B. Who?

Bob. Rose and Polly Dowler.

B. Hum! Indeed! (*Voices heard outside.*) Bob, I hear Miss Milford. Go, at once! I want to speak to her. (*Exit Bob L.*) I'll soon see who is to win her. She is worth a struggle.

Enter Rose, *R.*

R. Good afternoon, Miss Milford!

R. Good afternoon, Mr. Brantford!

B. I have not seen you for some time. You improve every day.

R. (*Seating herself by table.*) Indeed!

B. (*Seating himself opposite.*) Quite true! No empty compliments I assure you. The rose on the mountain is not more lovely than its namesake in the valley.

R. Mr. Brantford, a neat compliment from a friend is always acceptable to a woman, but wholesale praises lack as much in true politeness as they do in good taste. (*Rises.*)

B. Really, I expressed only the admiration that I feel. I had hoped that my long acquaintance with your estimable father, and my frequent visits here justified me in saying so. In fact, I have not told half the admiration I feel.

R. (*Hastily.*) No further explanation is necessary. Your apology is ample. I presume you wish to see my mother on business.

B. (*Aside.*) *Apology!* Hang it! (*Aloud.*) Now, Miss Rose, isn't it too hard to condemn a fellow to talk business forever? (*Laughs.*) Surely it is! I wish to converse with you on a more agreeable subject. I want a wife. It is a little sudden, but I'll give you time to think over it.

R. Mr. Brantford, I am surprised at such an avowal from your lips. There is no need for time to reflect. It can never be.

B. Oh, don't be in a hurry about deciding. Such things require time.

R. (*Spiritedly.*) But I say it requires no time. I beg of you, Mr. Brantford, that you will never mention this subject to me again.

B. I see some trifling objections to such a match. But the advantages, I think, overbalance them. True, I am some twenty years older than you, but I think I am a pretty good man yet, and there may be worse looking fellows of twenty-five.

R. I was not thinking of your *years* at all. Mr. Brantford, this is not a pleasant subject.

B. Something of a surprise, of course! So we'll just defer it, with a few more words. As for love, I do not see that it differs from mere sentiment, and sentiment in matrimony is not half as good as common sense. I esteem you very highly and I have no doubt you would, in time, think me a model husband. You have money, so have I.

R. No more, sir! Mr. Brantford, you compel me to do what I otherwise should never have done; I don't like you. Let me tell you once for all, that I despise you.

B. (*Nettled.*) *Despise!* Ah, you are a trifle sarcastic, I think.

R. You wrung it from me,

B. You are young, and I forgive you. The time may come when you will change your mind. Think it over.

Enter Mrs. M. R.

Good bye, Rose! (*Seizes her hand and kisses it. Does not see Mrs. M.*)

R. Mr. Brantford! (*B. exits suddenly L. saying "Good bye."*)

Mrs. M. (*Severely.*) Rose, what is this?

R. (*Startled.*) Oh! Is it you, mother?

Mrs. M. Yes, it is I. And a pretty sight I see! A young lady in her teens and supposed to be the pink of propriety, allowing a man old enough to be her father, to kiss her on the sly. For shame!

R. Indeed, it was all a mistake, mother.

Mrs. M. A great mistake! I grant it. (*Aside.*) So I have a rival in this upstart girl. (*Aloud.*) You shall repent this folly, Rose.

R. Mother, please listen, nothing was meant.

Mrs. M. Of course, it usually means nothing when middle-aged men kiss girls young enough to be their daughters. (*Angrily.*) So unwomanly an act can not be explained. I have learned at last, what your false modesty is worth, girl.

R. Mother, you are cruel and unjust. (*Bursts into tears.*) Oh, father, if you only knew the trials and sorrows of your orphan child. (*Drops into a chair and leans her head on the table weeping.*) I wish I were in my grave, too.

Mrs. M. Tears are useless to wash away stains!

R. (*Rising proudly and very erect, speaks with pride and dignity.*) Stains! Mrs. Milford, who dares to speak to me of stains?

Mrs. M. I, your guardian! It is my duty to watch over you. Be careful you do not step beyond the boundary of obedience. I have the power to punish.

R. I admit your power to punish, Mrs. Milford, but remember it is also your duty to enquire before you judge so harshly. I know not why, but your chastening seems more like vengeance than the discipline of a kind guardian. Our lives must henceforth be apart, but remember, a higher power shall judge between us, and that power has said, "Vengeance is mine, I will repay, saith the Lord."

TABLEAU.

Mrs. M. R C, Rose facing her L C, with right arm extended pointing towards Mrs. M. but a little to the right of her, Mrs. M. with anger in her eyes looking directly at Rose.

ACT II.

SCENE.—*Same as in Act I. Time, a few days after Act I. Polly showing in Brantford as curtain rises.*

P. Take a seat, Mr. Brantford. I will call Mrs. Milford. (*Exit P., R. B. seats himself.*)

B. (*Tapping his boot with riding whip.*) What a cosy place this is. I think I shall move in here myself some day. The day need not be far distant, either, if I consulted only the mistress of the house. Hark! She comes now. (*Lays his whip aside.*)

Enter MRS. MILFORD, *R.*

Mrs. M. Ah, Mr. Brantford, you are punctual to your appointment I see. (*Mrs. M. seats herself O near him.*)

B. Yes, but don't you give me any credit for it, Mrs. Milford. Punctuality is second nature with me. I am a business man, you know.

Mrs. M. (*Laughs.*) Please do not mention business for once. We all know you are a business man.

B. Now, Mrs. Milford, don't be too hard on the devotee to business. You are unnecessarily cruel. You know I have changed the old proverb "Business before pleasure" into "Business is pleasure."

Mrs. M. Oh, indeed! Then I would not deprive you of a single pleasure for the world and will humor your whim.

B. Now, don't say *whim*. Really, that is too hard on a fellow.

Mrs. M. Then I amend it, and say a little pet conceit.

B. Yes, yes! fix it as you will. Suit yourself.

Mrs. M. You don't know how happy I am since the worry of settling that will case is over. I knew the court would set that will aside.

B. Exactly! They couldn't help it. And I am also delighted to have the result so agreeable to you. How does Miss Rose take the decision which strips her all at once of all her property.

Mrs. M. I am surprised at the indifference of this girl. She actually seems to care nothing for money. I cannot understand it at all.

B. Indeed! Very philosophic I would say, but very impractical. What does the young man say?

Mrs. M. He doesn't seem to care, either, but that is easily accounted for, as he got nothing, anyway.

B. As guardian of Miss Rose, of course you will make *some* provision for her education. I suppose she will have a home with you?

Mrs. M. Yes, she is welcome to stay here, though I think something of sending her to Col. Warley's. They want a servant, a sort of governess and lady's maid, and all sorts.

B. (*Surprised.*) Yes, especially all sorts! That's decidedly good! Mrs. Milford, that I think would not be advisable under the circumstances.

Mrs. M. You speak of education. Is not the most necessary education a young lady can have, that which gives her the power of taking care of herself?

B. Very true, but the step you contemplate is unnecessary. Have you thought that the service at Col. Warley's is hard and the pay poor?

Mrs. M. People who earn their bread are not always able to say where they shall get it.

B. This I think is an exception, Mrs. Milford. I beg your pardon, but I have been acquainted with your family so long, that I feel free to offer advice. I do not advise this step. The events of this lawsuit are still fresh in the minds of the community. Some feeling is aroused, and such things are better forgotten. Your husband was a power in this country. He always treated the Mountain Rose, as the girl is called, as his own child. It might be well to make no sudden changes in her station.

Mrs. M. I have considered all that. I am her lawful guardian and shall do as I please with her. I thought the place a good enough one for her.

B. Why not keep her as your own maid?

Mrs. M. I need no maid. If she stays here she must go into the kitchen with the servants. I think I shall send her to Col. Warley's.

B. Mrs. Milford, I hope it may not seem presumption if I remind you that I have lately performed services for you that no one else could perform.

Mrs. M. You have my sincerest gratitude.

B. You contemplate making extensive improvements to your mansion and on the plantation. A few days ago I negotiated a large loan for you.

Mrs. M. You took a mortgage for it. No further obligations are due there.

B. Yes, I *do* hold a mortgage on the estate. I do not wish to be unpleasant, but would it not be well to grant the man who has done so much one trifling favor?

Mrs. M. Then you wish the girl to remain!

B. I do.

Mrs. M. She shall but not as *lady's maid*.

B. Doubtless she will much prefer to remain here for less compensation and possibly fewer privileges. By the way, how do you like that new cook I sent you?

Mrs. M. Miss Button is an excellent servant. She is very

industrious. Her brother, Bob, is a first rate man at farm work, and reliable, too, I think.

Enter FRANK, *R.*

F. I beg pardon Mrs. Milford. Do I intrude?

Mrs. M. Oh, no! come in! I will go to the library at once and write that letter of recommendation for you. I forgot it entirely. (*Exit, L.*)

B. So you are off at last, Mr. Colewood?

F. Yes, at *last.*

B. Doubtless you are anxious to test your powers in life's struggle.

F. I am not at all anxious to test my powers with anybody, Mr. Brantford, but should the circumstances demand it, I will do my best.

B. (*With a sneer.*) Young men are always enthusiastic.

F. And unfortunately they are too often confiding. But after all a young man's enthusiasm may be a match for an old man's duplicity.

B. Sir, your language is not very clear; but I understand it has been clear at times. You talked a little too much about the way the affairs of Mr. Milford's estate were adjusted. That was doubtless due to disappointment, but my advice is to be cautious.

F. My relations to Mr. Milford's family entitled me to an opinion. My sentiments are my own; I'll speak them when I please, Ky. Brantford, and defend them if necessary.

B. Nonsense, boy! I'll not bandy words with you. Don't you know I could have you put—well, no matter where, inside of twenty-four hours?

F. Oh, I've heard that masked men ride through the mountains at your call. Because the "Regulators" are at your back you feel safe in insulting helpless women. Go slow, Ky. Brantford! justice may overtake you yet.

B. (*Quickly.*) Women! Who made you a defender of women?

F. The God who gave me a strong right arm, just as he made every true man a defender of woman. (*Scornfully.*) Bah! the man who will impose on a woman because God made him stronger than she is too contemptible to live.

B. I can't see, Mr. Colewood, what these fine moral sentiments are all about, jealousy possibly inspires them. Jealousy is a bitter passion to nourish. Other scenes will do you good, so I wish you a swift journey, and for the good of your health I advise you to settle outside of the state.

F. I'll settle where I please and ask your advice when I want it. Sometime I hope to offer you a little. (*Exit, L.*)

B. The young scamp! He means mischief. I'll take some of that conceit out of him, I warrant, before he is aware of it.

Enter ROSE, *R.*

R. Excuse me, Mr. Brantford, I thought mother was here.

B. Mrs. Milford is in the library for a moment. Sit down, Miss Milford. I just called on a little matter of business to-day. Among other things your name was mentioned. Mrs. Milford thought of getting you a situation as lady's maid but I persuaded her to let you remain here.

R. Oh, thank you, Mr. Brantford. I am so glad. I am so attached to the old home.

B. So I thought. It should still be your home.

R. I will remember your kindness, Mr. Brantford. (*Exit L.*)

B. Gad! I'll excite her gratitude, and a woman's gratitude is not to be despised. I'll get that Frank out of the way and then all is safe. The widow's eyes will gradually open to the situation when it is too late for her to do anything but make the best of it. Now I must find Bob, and devise a safe plan for disposing of Frank. (*Exit R.*)

Enter MRS. M. *and* ROSE, *L.*

R. Mother, I am so glad you have decided that I shall remain here; I so dearly love the old homestead. Why did you not employ Frank again instead of a stranger?

Mrs. M. I thought it best that he should go. Please ask no questions. As for yourself, you need not waste many thanks. I can do nothing better for you than to teach you to work.

R. With that I am content for the present, if I stay in the dear old home.

Mrs. M. I can promise nothing better for the future. But we will say no more on that subject. I heard you speaking with Mr. Brantford. What was he saying to you?

R. Nothing, but that he had persuaded you to let me live here.

Mrs. M. And what did you say to him?

R. I thanked him for his kindness.

Mrs. M. And did your gratitude cause the glow on your cheeks when you came to me?

R. Mother!

Mrs. M. Do not strive to conceal anything, I see it all. Your conduct is shameful. How dare you aspire to one so far above you?

R. Oh, mother! mother! How can you speak so? There is nothing between Mr. Brantford and me. You know I dislike him.

Mrs. M. But would like his fortune. Do not call me mother. I would be ashamed of such a child.

R. (*Sadly, but with dignity.*) It is hard to forget the tender terms of happier days. But I will never call you mother again. I loved you as one and hoped to win your love. My heart yearned for a mother's love. But I never knew it. I am only Rose Milford and you are my legal guardian.

Mrs. M. And as your guardian, I shall see that you occupy your proper sphere. As you remain here, you had better enter at once into your new duties. (*Rings bell.*) Where is Mr. Brantford?

R. I left him here.

Enter SOOKY BUTTON, *R.*

Mrs. M. Miss Button, you will hereafter assign work to Rose in the kitchen.

Sooky. Yes, ma'am. (*Pronounce the a flat. Hesitates.*) What natur' o' work?

Mrs. M. Let her scour and clean.

S. But Polly and the colored girl can do all that.

Mrs. M. Do as you are bid! If there is not enough work for all, Polly may do chamber work.

S. Laws a me, ma'am, I never thought of disobeyin' orders. There's right amart o' work, an' I reckon I'll find plenty that's hard enough.

Mrs. M. You understand my wishes I see. You may go.

S. Yes, ma'am! (*Exit, R.*)

Mrs. M. (*Aside.*) We'll see if he makes love to a kitchen girl. (*Aloud.*) Rose, you will be taught housekeeping. It is best for you. Sooky will expect obedience.

R. I have never yet disobeyed. (*Exit Mrs. M, L.*) Only a servant! 'Tis a cruel, cruel ending of bright visions of the future. A few weeks ago I was heiress to a large estate, to-day a penniless domestic. Better that I had never known wealth. I asked it not but the fates thrust it upon me in mockery to take it away again and taunt me with my misery. Oh father, it.was a cruel blow that took you from the child you loved and left the orphan in the care of one you trusted. How I loved that woman; but she spurns my love. Oh hate, I must choke you down or you will rise in my heart. Even Frank, the brother of my childhood is cold, and leaves me to my fate. I who loved him so.

Enter POLLY *and* IKE *unobserved, R.*

R. Deserted by every one, I am indeed friendless and alone (*Bursts into tears.*)

P. No, Rose, you are not friendless while I live. (*Soothes her.*) Cheer up, you still have friends, if they are poor.

I. Polly, tell her I'm here too.

R. Thank you, Polly, and you too, Mr. Hopper. I am so glad that you do not forget me.

P. It's just as mean as can be sending you to the kitchen, and to have that Sooky Button for boss. (*Stamps her foot.*) I'd like to strangle her, so I would.

I. Now, Polly, be keerful how you talk. You have no idee how stranglin' hurts. Onc't I got into a 'lection row down at Cliffville, an' two big fellers held me while another choked me. I felt sorter like a court-house was a sottin' on top of me. I reckon I'd felt right smart wuss than I did if our side hadn't got the upper hand pretty soon.

P. I'd choke her, see if I wouldn't. She's mean as pusley and Mrs. Milford isn't much better.

R. Polly, it is not proper to speak so about the mistress of the house.

P. I can't help it!

I. Miss Rose, I ain't much of a hand for fine words an' I can't say that I'm exactly a ladies' man sich as the novels read about but if you ever need a friend for rough knocks, jest call on Ike Hopper.

R. Mr. Hopper,—

I. Jest say Ike.

R. Well then, Ike, I shall not forget you, I assure you.

I. Now Polly, Sooky will be arter you pretty soon.

P. Humph! Let her come.

Enter ZEKE, R.

Z. I golly, dis is de blightin'est shame I ever seen. It's a disgrace onto de county to take every dollar Miss Rose ebber had an' den put her into de kitchen 'long wid de niggers and de poor white trash dat ain't fit to black her shoes; no dey hain't fit to black a black's shoes.

R. Never mind that now, Zeke. It was according to law and I suppose it is right.

Z. Tain't right, if it is law. De law is wusser'n de small pox. Dah's Massa Frank, he's gwine away dis evenin, without gettin' his own. Whar's de law in dat! He's desperit blue 'bout it. Whah's de law or de jestiss?

R. (*With interest.*) Is Frank sorry to leave!

Z. I golly, Missa, he feels jist as if he'd taken a whole handful of blue pills an' couldn't dijist 'em. Does for a fac.

I. His feelings must be allfired strong then, I reckon.

Z. Powerful strong; strong as garlic or sour kraut!

P. I wish I was a man!

Z. Mebbe de same 'ud happen you as did my brother Mose when he was born.

P. What was that!

Z. Doan know as I oughter tell it.

P. Then don't!

I. Yes, Zeke, tell us!

Z.   Massa Ike, it was pooty tough on Mose.

I.   Out with it.

Z.   He was *tongue tied!*

P.   You mean thing!

Z.   You see Miss Polly, you oughter wished you wus a white man; case if you'd been a nigger you'd had to wish over agin. Tell you if I was a white man I'd chaw up sumfin.

I.   A chicken bone, Zeke?

Z.   No sir'ee, I'd bite off a few *buttons!* Dat Sooky Button she says she says, Zeke, git de brick dust. So she got all de knives an' de forks. I says yes, Missa Button, I'll skyower de knives; an' she says, no, Rose 'ill do de skyowerin'. I was so mad I nearly said sumfin' but I didn't.

I.   Why didn't you? Darkies are free now.

Z.   (*Shakes his head.*) No, sar! I jest slipped de knives an' forks into de wood shed an' polished 'em up. Missa Rose won't do no skyowerin' while Zeke is roun'.

R.   Thank you, Zeke, you are very kind.

Enter SOOKY, *R.*

S.   Polly, your work is suffering in the kitchen.

P.   What if it is? I'll find it out myself.

S.   I shall report you to Mrs. Milford for neglect.

P.   Do if you dare, Sooky Button. I know my place and my business. There *are* some things I can report too.

S.   Work must not be neglected. Rose, you will scour all the cutlery at once. It's a right smart job an' you'd better be at it at onc't. When I've a job to do I do it, an' no laggin'.

Z.   (*Aside.*) I golly, so do I, if it's an easy job.

I.   Miss Button, I reckon you're some on house work.

S.   (*Taking it as a compliment.*) I pride myself that I am, Mr. Hopper.

Z.   Missa Button am a reg'lar—reg'lar—a reg'lar gineral in de kitchen.

S.   Zeke, I'd teach you to mind your own business if I was boss on the plantation. Bob's too easy on you. Listenin' is manners, when betters is talkin'.

Z.   Golly! I 'spose Missa done tole you dat.

S.   (*Snappishly.*) Humph! I reckon I was brought up to know that. Girl, come to your work. (*Exeunt, Sooky, Polly, followed by Zeke and Ike R.*)

R.   What a very disagreeable woman. I shall let her get no advantage of me. She is a spy for her precious brother Bob, in my opinion. Frank leaves soon, I hope he will come now to bid me good bye. His absence is hardest of all to bear. But he is right in choosing another field for his splendid talents. I hear his footsteps now.

Enter FRANK, *L.*

F. Rose, everything is ready and I shall start in time to reach Cliffville to-night,

R. Frank, I am so sorry you are going.

F. And I am pained to leave you in such distressing circum-stances. A few months have made great changes. I don't care for myself. A man can make his way anywhere.

R. You are sure to succeed, Frank, and when success crowns your efforts, think sometimes of the sister you left behind whose best wishes will always be with you.

F. Rose, your kindness encourages me to say something which I had never intended to say. If I make a mistake forgive me, is all I ask. I must tell you, Rose, how I love you. Do you care for me?

R. Dear Frank, I have always loved you.

F. How stupid I have been! But your words, dear Rose, will make my journey light.

R. And yours will cheer my lowly station here. Come what may, I care not, for old friends are best after all.

F. That I shall never forget. But time presses. The horses are saddled and I suppose Zeke is ready. Dear Rose, remember you have enemies here and also trusty friends. Be on your guard. I have secured a good place in the adjoining county where I can watch over your safety. Confide in Ike Hopper. He will be a true friend. I will write to you, and when you are free, will come to claim you for my wife. Adieu! We'll meet soon, possibly. The thought of your love will cheer my hours of toil. (*Kisses her.*)

R. Good bye, Frank; God bless you. (*Exit Frank, L.*) Then he has not forgotten me because of my misfortunes. I wronged him cruelly. He is too noble for that.

Enter BOB BUTTON, *R.*

Bob. Good evenin', Rose.

R. (*Aside.*) The insolence! (*Aloud.*) What did you want, Mr. Button?

Bob. Oh, I didn't want nothin'. I was goin' to get a chair to fix in the library, so I reckoned I'd chat a spell.

R. (*Curtly.*) I do not care to chat just now.

Bob. Well, sometimes I feel that'y, too, but I 'low us hired folks ort to get acquainted. Sister Sookey says I'm a great feller to get acquainted with the girls.

R. (*With temper.*) Mr. Button, gentlemen are not usually in such a hurry getting acquainted with young ladies. (*Exit, L.*)

Bob. Huffed, by jiminy! Well, young lady, I 'sposed one hired hand was as good as another, an' mebbe you'll live to think so, too.

Enter BRANTFORD, R.

B. I've been looking for you, Bob.

Bob. Well, here I am. What's wanted?

B. Now, since young Colewood is going, he may have some plan for eloping with that girl. Keep the big brown horse in the stable ready to saddle at a moment's notice. Keep your eyes open. If she escapes, bring her back. There's danger—in it. Will you undertake the job?

Bob. It's just what I'd like. You can bet on me. (*Aside.*) Just the thing for me! I'd bring her back purty lively.

B. All right, but in order to make sure, I think the Regulators ought to meet at the old cabin to-morrow night. Frank Colewood refuses to leave the state. We'll try a little moral suasion. (*They move to the left while talking.*)

Enter POLLY, R, *unobserved. She withdraws behind the door and listens.*

Bob. On the usual charge of horse stealin', I 'spose?

B. Yes, that's safest now. He knows that means a rope unless he leaves at once.

Bob. Then I am to notify the Regulators?

B. Yes! (*Exeunt, L.*)

P. The miserable villains. Horse stealin' means hangin' in this country. I'll beat them yet. If Ike was only here. (*Exit hastily, R.*)

CURTAIN.

ACT III.

SCENE I.—*The haunted cabin in the mountains. Meeting of the Regulators. A deserted cabin. Plain bench, R. Chimney, L. Door in flat, C. Enter* IKE *and* ZEKE. *Evening. Stage dark.*

I. Now, Zeke, look out for ghosts!

Z. I golly, Massa Ike, don't mention ghosts. Dat's a solumn subjec'. (*Keeps close to Ike.*)

I. Say, Zeke, won't you just go around the corner of the house and look for that headless man who has his headquarters here? They say he's about ten feet high.

Z. (*Frightened.*) Massa, keep still. Don't mention evil spirits. If you do dey'll come shuah! Shh! listen!

I. It's only the moaning of the wind, Zeke. We must be spry and hide ourselves. The Regulators will be here as soon as it gets a little darker. Now, Zeke, screw up your courage. If you fail we may both lose our lives if discovered. Don't let any ghost nonsense scare you.

Z. Fore de Lord, dis ain't no funny business! But dis nigger'll take keer o' hisself if dat ten feet man with no head'll tend his own business.

I. I will climb this big chimney and rest on the jambs. I can hear all that happens on the inside of the cabin. You must hide yourself in the laurel thicket, and see if any parties leave before the others and where they go. Can you do it?*

Z. Yes, sah! Shh! shh! (*They listen.*)

I. They are coming now! Quick, Zeke! (*Zeke exits hastily and Ike disappears up the chimney.*)

Enter KY., BOB *and other Regulators in masks.* KY. *and* BOB *remove their masks and talk, O front.*

B. Did the Bear Creek boys say that they would turn out?

Bob. Some of 'em will, but we don't need many. The thing will be a complete surprise.

B. Colewood is stopping at Judge Arman's across the river Don't fail. He must be in the lock-up at Cliffville to-night, then if anything happens him why nobody will be surprised. Do you think there will be any attempt at a rescue?

Bob. No, I 'low not. Nobody'll know till it's all over. To-night about ten o'clock will be the time I suppose?

B. Yes; how many men are outside with Myer?

Bob. Five.

B. (*Turning to others, some of whom are conversing in low tones.*) Men, of course you understand our business. Frank Colewood is suspected of horse stealing. For the present he is to be put in the county jail. You had better mount. Myer will lead you. (*Exit, all but Bob and Ky.*) Button, you had better burn that list of friendly Regulators I gave you.

Bob. I 'low so. (*Produces match and paper. Sets it on fire and throws it into the chimney and turns away.*) I don't like papers, Ky., they blab sometimes.

B. Neither do I like them. Hist! I hear hoofs. It is the Bear Creek boys. (*Notices fire blazing in the chimney caught in rubbish.*) I declare, that chimney's afire. You are very careless, Bob.

Bob. Listen! I could swear I heard a noise on the roof. (*The fire burns down.*)

B. I think it was the boys outside, still I'll make sure. (*Exits to look.*)

---

*In case it is impossible to represent a fire-place on the stage, Ike may say he is going outside to climb down the chimney, or a screen may represent a projection in the wall behind which he may conceal himself.

Bob. It sounded as if it was in the chimney. (*Peers up chimney.*) Dark as a stack o' black cats! Don't like haunted houses. (*B. re-enters.*)

B. It's all right. It wasn't even the headless man. An owl flew from the roof just as I started out.

Bob. I think that was a good chunk of an owl to make such a noise.

B. Come, the boys are all ready. (*Exeunt.*)

Enter IKE, *stealthily.*

I. That was a close call! The dirty cut-throats, they tried to roast me! That owl was sent by Providence, I reckon.

Enter ZEKE, *badly scared.*

Z. I's done got enough of dis yar night's soldjerin. One o' dem Bear Creek fellers cut across lots an' nearly rode plumb over me as I laid in the bushes.

I. The villains tried to roast me.

Z. Lordy, you's jokin', Ike!

I. They fired the chimney and I scampered lively to the roof. When they ran outside to see what made the noise, an owl flew away. Zeke, I wouldn't shoot that owl for a thousand dollars.

Z. Dat owl was a disposition of Providence. Nothin' short of de Lord A'mighty could o' saved you. Yes, sah, a disposition of Providence.

I. How many were there of them, Zeke?

Z. About twenty.

I. I heard it nearly all. They will arrest Frank at the Judge's, and take him to the lock-up at Cliffville. Since the jail burnt they put the prisoners in a crazy old log house. We'll take him out safe. We'll ride home and tell the Mountain Rose not to worry. We can ride to Cliffville in two hours easy.

Z. I'm 'fraid der's somefin' goin' to happen. I dreamed las' night dat a big black snake long as a pastur' lot was tryin' to swaller de biggest kind of a black tom cat. Dat's a bad sign.

I. Yes, for the cat.

Z. I tell you dere's somefin' in dat dream.

I. Suet pudden', Zeke.

Z. Ike, ef we takes Massa Frank from de Reg'lators I'm 'fraid dere'll be more'n suet pudding, dere'll be mince meat.

I. All right, Zeke, I'll risk it. Come on. (*Leads out.*)

CURTAIN

SCENE II.—*The Cliffville log jail. Wooden bench. A dim tallow candle burning stuck in a bottle. A lounge bed, R, and an old chair. Door in flat, C. Frank a prisoner. Moonlight through chinks and grating.*

F. (*Seated, C.*) They sprung their trap a little sooner than I expected, and nipped me. The worst has not come yet. The community is excited, and a man charged with horse stealing has no opportunity to prove his innocence. Judge Lynch's court is in frequent session lately. A designing enemy may cause the death of an innocent man. That I have bitter, unscrupulous enemies I well know. To die on a tree! To be hung like a dog! (*Shudders*) ugh! it is too horrible to contemplate. No, I will make one last effort to save *her* that disgrace. (*Rises and looks around.*) The moonlight through the chinks! Ah, I had forgotten that this is not the old brick jail. Precious time is already wasted. (*Peers out.*) It is past midnight and a terrible storm is gathering on the mountains. How vivid that lightning is in the distance. The moon will soon be obscured. So much the better. Escape is then easy. (*Frank tries the door and the grating, then examines the walls. The moon vanishes and total darkness ensues. Soon a flash of lightning.*) Some one approaches! (*Clasps his forehead.*) Oh, God, it is too late! (*A flash of lightning and a peal of thunder. Noise of unlocking the door. The door opens and Bob Button enters masked. He closes the door after him.*) Are you friend or foe?

Bob. (*Throwing off mask.*) Look for yourself.

F. Bob Button! What do you want?

Bob. Your life is in my hands.

F. That may be, but remember it is not always safe to push a man at bay too far.

Bob. Keep still! (*Draws near and speaks in low tone.*) 'Tween you and me, I don't like Ky. Brantford a bit better than you do, an' I've no grudge agin you. You always treated me white. The Regulators that put you here didn't do it for nothin'. They say you're a horse thief.

F. They are liars! (*Continued thunder and lightning with gusts of rain.*)

Bob. Oh, keep still! It'll pay you to listen. They'll be here in a half an hour. I'll tell you what I'll do. I'll let you out for fifty dollars. You can give 'em the slip and skip the country.

F. I haven't half that amount, Bob.

Bob. I can't take the risk for nothin'. Now you'd better shell out. There's no gettin' away.

F. But I haven't the money. I have but ten dollars.

Bob. That ain't likely. Mrs. Milford paid you over a hundred dollars.

F. I am telling you the truth. I disposed of the money. I will send it to you if you will trust me.

Bob. The Regulators don't do a credit business. If you are fool enough to be hung, all right. It's a pity to hang you with all that money in your pocket. Then it will be divided, so I'll just take my share now. Pull off that coat and vest till I look at the pockets.

F. Never! I told you the truth; if I must die, I'll die in defence of my rights. (*Pulls a pocket knife.*)

Bob. Humph! I thought they took all your weepons, but I see they left you a tooth-pick. Curse it, I'd shoot you and make short work of it if it wasn't for raisin' an alarm. (*Pulls immense bowie knife.*) Now, lay down that ar knife and behave yourself, or I'll slice some bumps off you.

F. Take this knife if you want it. (*Bob advances cautiously and thrusts at Frank who skillfully parries. Frank has hastily wrapped a large silk handkerchief around his hand which enables him to parry safely. Bob gradually gets excited while Frank is cool.*)

Bob. Curse that handkerchief! (*Frank gradually works around till he is directly in front of the old chair. Bob makes a desperate pass which Frank avoids by jumping aside. Frank seizes the chair and before Bob can recover, knocks him senseless and rushes out knocking over the candle. Lighting and heavy peal of thunder.*)

Enter ROSE *excitedly after a short pause.*

R. Oh, I am too late! too late! the villain has killed him and escaped! (*Wrings her hands helplessly.*) What shall I do! (*Bob moans.*) He is not dead! Speak to me, Frank! (*Bob rises and gets the candle.*)

Bob. (*Gruffly.*) Who's there?

R. That is not his voice. Where is he?

Bob. (*Lights candle.*) Oho, my pretty one, the Mountain Rose is out late at night.

R. (*Screams.*) I am betrayed!

Bob. Keep still! No screams here! You gave me a lesson in manners onc't, now I'll give you one.

R. Where is Frank Colewood?

Bob. He jest stepped out to jine some friends, but I reckon I don't complain of losin' his company seein' I've got a good deal better. Come, sit down and rest yourself. (*Takes her by the arm to lead her to the bench.*)

R. Bob Button, don't you dare lay hands on me! (*Pushing him off with spirit.*)

Bob. Miss, 'praps you better not forgit you are not at home now. Be keerful of your temper.

R. (*Sinking on the bench and covering her face with her hands.*) Oh dear! I'm lost. Oh please let me go! How can you be so cruel!

Bob. By jimminy, she's goin' to faint. I don't know what to do with a faintin' woman. (*Tries to soothe her.*) Rose, you needn't be skeered so bad. Come, sit up. (*Tries to remove her hands from her face.*) Stop yer poutin', can't yer? Nobody's hurtin' you.

Enter suddenly IKE *and* ZEKE.

I. Hands off, scoundrel. (*Knocks Bob violently across the room.*) Is there no man about you?

Bob. I wasn't doin' any harm !

I. You're a mean skulkin' varmint. There is the door ! Now git ! (*Draws pistol on Bob; Bob starts toward the door.*) Zeke, hadn't I better give him our compliments? (*Kicks Bob as he goes out.*)

Z. Dat's right, Massa Ike. Always give gentlemen your respects as dey leave. We's done got here right in de pint o' time. In two minnits more it'ud been too late to be soon enough.

R. Ike, you have saved me!

I. Miss Rose, it was very unwise for you to attempt Frank's rescue. You should have left that to Zeke and me.

R. I couldn't bear to stay at home when I feared he might be killed. I came across the hills and beat you.

I. Brave, but reckless !

Z. Dat hill road's like ridin' up a tree an' gallopin' on de top of it. Didn't break your neck or nuffin?

R. (*Laughing.*) No, Zeke, I came through perfectly sound.

I. We must be off, the whole gang will be down on us in ten minutes. We will separate. Hurry up, there is not a moment to lose. (*Exeunt.*)

CURTAIN.

ACT IV.

SCENE.—*Mrs. Milford's. Mrs. M. seated by window reading.*

Mrs. M. I wonder where Button was last night? His nocturnal rides are a little mysterious. I must enquire into them. (*She rings bell for Polly.*)

Enter POLLY, *R.*

Mrs. M. Polly, has Robert finished his work in the garden?

P. Not yet, ma'am. He is'nt feelin' well to-day and complains of a bad headache.

Mrs. M. Tell him I wish to see him.

P. Yes, ma'am! (*Exit R.*)

Mrs. M. It is not strange that men have headaches when they are out so late riding over the country. It is unaccountable that Robert's business calls him away so frequently.

Enter Bob, *R., head bandaged with handkerchief.*

Bob. Did you want to see me, ma'am?

Mrs. M. Polly says you are complaining of a headache to-day.

Bob. (*Uneasy.*) Yes, ma'am. I never have had it before so bad.

Mrs. M. You were away very late last night. I heard hoofs on the drive some time after midnight.

Bob. Yes, I wanted to see a man down at Cliff Court House, but could not find him till very late.

Mrs. M. Doubtless loss of sleep caused your headache. If possible I should prefer to have my men at home sooner. Parties are abroad sometimes intent on violence and your absence may cause suspicion to fall on us.

Bob. Yes, ma'am. I'll try to be in earlier, after this.

Mrs. M. There is a liniment somewhere about the house that will help you. I will have Polly find it. You will feel better if you remove that handkerchief, I think.

Bob. (*Hastily.*) Oh, you needn't git any liniment. It's gettin' better now.

Mrs. M. A little will do no harm! (*Exit R.*)

Bob. Hang it, if she gits to foolin' round my head the cat's out o' the bag sure. An' there *are* folks who don't approve of last night's doin's.

Enter Rose, *R.*

Bob. Say, Rose, don't you tell what happened last night.

R. You are not so brave, Mr. Button, as you were then.

Bob. I reckon it might look jest as bad for you as for me. I didn't do anything outen the way, did I?

R. Nothing but try to murder an unarmed man and insult a woman, whom accident placed in your power.

Bob. Hush, can't yer! There's Ike and Zeke. I kin make it purty hot for them. If you tell I'll tell. Ky Brantford will have them both discharged and run out o' the country.

R. I shan't tell!

Bob. All right! Rose, let's be friends. I've tried to be friends with you. I know I'm not exactly as good as I might be, but somehow I always feel as if I could be better if you would only think well of me.

R. The man who would wrong a woman who is in his power, is as bad as a murderer. Your life would not be safe if my friends knew of your baseness.

Bob. Don't tell, Miss Rose, and I'll never trouble you again. Don't tell Ike.

R. I will say nothing on condition you never speak to me again, except when your duties make it necessary.

Bob. (*Doggedly.*) I'll try, Miss Rose! I'll do anything for you!
R. (*Going aside.*) He is not so bold now, the poor coward.
(*Exit, L.*)
Bob. I s'pose I am a fool for carin' for her, and a scamp too,
for that matter. I've never had much chance to be anything an'
she was rich and educated. But I can't help likin' her she's so
pretty. I'd a'most try to be good if she'd marry me. I'm a fool.
She's so proud an' don't care any more for me than she does for a
toad. But mebbe I'll git her yet sometime an' she had better
make a friend of me than an enemy.

Enter Ky., *L.*

B. Oho, Bob, I hardly expected to find an able-bodied over-
seer in the house this fine afternoon. What's the matter, eh?
Bob. Headache!
B. Late hours! (*Laughs.*)
Bob. Yes, losin' sleep hurts me mor'n it used to.
B. This affair has caused considerable talk. Colewood has a
good many friends. We must keep still. How did you man-
age it?
Bob. I follered orders. I went to the jailer an' got the key.
I unlocked the jail an' told Frank I came as a friend an' that he
might take his choice, leave the country or swing.
B. So he concluded to leave?
Bob. He left suddint, curse him!
B. Hopper knows too much about this affair. Frank must
have seen him since he got out!
Bob. I reckon not.
B. I'm sure of it. They have laid some plans. Keep a close
watch. Rose may try to escape.
Bob. (*Savagely.*) See if I don't look out for that.
B. If Hopper don't behave he'll leave the country too.
Bob. Tain't safe to fool with Hopper. He has a good many
friends among the Squirrel Hunters.
B. Button, don't be a coward.
Bob. See here, Ky. Brantford, it's not best for you to talk
about cowards. Where were you time of the war? Sneakin'
through the bushes, half union man half rebel but always a good
ways from danger.
B. You needn't talk! You were drafted!
Bob. If I was I didn't face ole Grant at Petersburg for nothin'.
I've smelled powder enough in ten minutes to make you sick for
three months—
B. All right, Bob, all right! But we mustn't talk here too
long. Be on your guard. (*Exit L.*)
Bob. Hanged if I'll risk my neck any longer to do his dirty
work. He don't care any more for a feller than he does for an'
old shoe in the road.

Enter POLLY *and* IKE, *R.*

P. Bob, I've found the liniment!

I. Want me to rub it on, Bob?

Bob. I wan't no liniment. Told yer I didn't want it.

I. Let me rub it on, Bob.

Bob. Hopper, 'tend to your own business an' I'll tend to mine. (*Aside.*) I'd break his head for a cent.

Enter ZEKE, *R.*

P. Ike, don't be too officious. Of course Mr. Button wants me to rub the liniment on his head.

Bob. (*Gruffly.*) I told you I wanted no liniment. Can't you let a fellow alone.

I. Zeke, can you tell what makes headache?

Z. De folks used to say dat ef you got youh haar cut an' de birds put it into der nests, dat makes headache.

I. For the birds?

Z. No, for the indivijal wot lost de haar!

P. Hasn't the atmosphere something to do with it?

Z. I 'spect de atmosphere may git out of order and make a big crop of headache. Ain't dat so, Massa Button?

Bob. Zeke, you're a darnation idiot, an' some day somebody'll hammer a little sense into you. (*Exit, R.*)

P. Ike, what does ail Bob's head?

I. It's a secret, Polly, isn't it, Zeke?

Z. A reg'lar blood-thirsty secret.

P. Oh, pshaw! tell me, I can keep it.

I. I'm afraid not, Polly.

P. Yes I can. Do tell me! I will make it easier for you to keep it.

I. How?

P. By helping you to keep it!

I. Well, I swear, Polly, I hadn't thought of that. I guess I'll confide in you, Polly. I'll tell you all I know. (*Pauses.*)

P. Well, go on!

I. I don't know anything about it myself, Polly.

P. That's a fib! Ike Hopper, I'd be ashamed to tell such stories.

I. I said it was a secret, didn't I?

P. Yes, and you said you'd tell me.

I. Well, if I don't know it, isn't it a secret as far as I am concerned? You see he had a little friendly set-to with Frank before we got there. I think that Frank must have knocked him down and hurt his head. He didn't say. We didn't injure his anatomy, did we Zeke?

Z. (*Rolls his eyes.*) I golly, Isaac, couldn't say. I didn't see his anatomy.

P. I'm so glad you spoiled their treacherous plans. Ike, what will be done next? We are still in danger. It's dreadful for Rose.

I. I know it, but I reckon they know by this time she has *some* friends. Frank hadn't time to say much while we talked in the cave, but he told us to keep a close watch. He will write, and if things get too bad, I'll agree with Zeke's help to take Rose where there's no danger. Frank will then marry her, and that will fix it I 'low, Polly.

Z. 'Spect that'll fix anybody!

P. Then you never could come back, Ike. The Regulators would make you scarce.

I. I wouldn't want to come back. You could follow, and maybe we could—

P. That will do, Mr. Hopper.

Z. I would settle dar, too. We'd get up a little exodus.

Enter SOOKY, *R.*

S. Polly, work's a sufferin'. You mustn't stay away so long. I could a took that liniment to town and back.

P. Then why didn't you take it?

S. Laws a me, I can't do everything. I never see'd such a set. Rose is gaddin' somewhere, too. Some folks ain't worth salt.

P. And some don't deserve salt.

S. It's small wages I'd pay if I were boss of this house. Polly, it's time supper was on the table, Mr. Brantford is here.

P. I'm coming! (*Exit S., R.*) The hateful old thing.

I. Polly, keep your temper, you may need it.

P. I do need it, and I use it every day lately, Ike.

I. For the benefit of your friends. (*Exeunt Polly, B, Ike and Zeke, L.*)

Enter ROSE, *L.*

R. I never can forget what Mr. Hopper has done for me, and Zeke, too. The poor black can be a true friend. Thank Heaven Frank is safe and I can brave their petty persecutions here. Oh, how I loathe and fear Bob Button; and not a friend I can confide in. She who should be my mother turns a deaf ear to all my appeals. I'll never ask a favor of her again. She is jealous of me. Goodness knows she is welcome to Ky. Brantford. I hate the sight of him. Did I hate her with mortal enmity, I could wish her no worse fate than to marry him. He is deep, dark and dangerous. My property will soon be his, and we shall all be beggars. Oh, God, why are such wrongs allowed to go unpunished!

Enter KY. BRANTFORD, *L.*

B. Ah, Miss Rose, I heard you passing in the hall and could not resist the temptation to drop in here.

R. Have a seat, Mr. Brantford.

B. (*Seats himself, L C.*) Take a seat yourself, Miss Milford. (*Rose seated R, at distance.*) Truly this is a delightful place. It does me so much good to visit here. Mr. Milford had an exquisite taste in selecting a site for his residence, and still better, if that were possible, in its adornment.

R. My father was a man of refined taste. Few men equalled him in *delicacy* and *refinement.*

B. Quite true! he was a man of culture. Culture gives refinement. Still, Miss Rose, do you not think that blunt men possess the sterner qualities of the man and gentleman in equal degree?

R. Possibly!

B. Possibly! That is not encouraging for the rest of us. It is very commendable of you under the circumstances, Miss Rose, to call Mr. Milford father.

R. (*With warmth.*) He was a true father to me. It was no fault of his that others defeated his wishes.

B. Things may not be so bad after all. Miss Milford, have you considered the question which we discussed some time since?

R. Mr. Brantford, I gave you my answer. It was a positive and final answer. Is it manly for you to persecute a helpless girl in this manner?

B. Young lady, I had hoped to find you in a more sensible mood. But then there is no hurry. You will change your mind yet. This family is in my power.

R. Mr. Brantford, have you no mercy?

B. Yes, for my friends—none for my enemies. Your pride shall be humbled, young woman. You shall be my wife. If not a happy, cheerful bride, then a sulking, handsome bride. Some women's hearts must be broken before you can do anything with them.

Enter IKE, *suddenly, R.*

I. Ky. Brantford (*Shaking his fist in his face*), you are brute!

B. And you are a sneaking eavesdropper! What right have you to skulk around trying to overhear the conversation of ladies and gentlemen?

I. I haven't overheard any *gentleman.*

B. Leave this room, Hopper, or I can't answer for the consequences.

I. I'll answer for them myself. I came here on an errand, and have as much right here as you have.

R. Gentlemen, please have no disturbance here.

B. Fellow, that excuse will not answer. If you came on an errand why do you wait to interrupt a private conversation?

I. I'll not stand and see a woman insulted while I can raise a hand in her defence. No man who claims to have a spark of manhood in him will act as you've done, Ky. Brantford. You're no gentleman.

B. (*Very angry.*) Take that back, Hopper, or I'll break your head. (*Advances threateningly.*)

I. That we can soon decide. (*Squares.*)

R. (*Excited, rushes between them.*) Please, gentlemen, remember where you are. Mr. Brantford, you forget yourself.

Enter MRS. M., R.

B. (*Cooling.*) I have been insulted.

Mrs. M. What is the matter, Mr. Brantford? This is a very strange scene. Mr. Hopper, did you want anything?

I. I just dropped in and Sooky Button asked me to go and find Polly.

Mrs. M. Then go at once, please. (*Exit Ike, L.*) Rose, will you please explain this extraordinary scene?

R. It is nothing.

Mrs. M. You may leave the room. I wish to speak with Mr. Brantford. (*Exit R, R.*) Now, Mr. Brantford, I wish to know exactly what the trouble is?

B. Hopper insulted me.

Mrs. M. I am very sorry. I shall reprimand him. I would not for a moment shield a servant in a matter like this, but had he no cause?

B. He overheard a remark that I made to Rose.

Mrs. M. May I enquire the subject of your conversation?

B. Yes! as her guardian I suppose you have a right to know I merely told her I wished her for my wife.

Mrs. M. (*Surprised.*) What! you can't mean it?

B. I do mean it.

Mrs. M. Have you considered this step? Have you considered her standing and yours?

B. I have considered everything, and shall marry the girl.

Mrs. M. Indeed! have you considered your relations to another person?

B. I have, and shall say to that other person now that she has built up false hopes upon insufficient grounds.

Mrs. M. (*Angrily.*) It is false, Ky. Brantford, you are guilty of double dealing. I know you at last, but I am not to be trifled with, remember.

B. Pshaw! I have made you no promises. There are no letters, drives or moonlight strolls. Don't try any breach of promise nonsense.

Mrs. M. But I have influence, and she shall never be your wife. You are not fit to be the husband of any true woman.

B. Humph! you have changed your mind very recently!

Mrs. M. Fool I was that I did not see it sooner. Everybody says you are a wretch, now I know it to be true.

B. Then if that fact is established, let us not discuss it further.

Mrs. M. I am Rose's guardian. I shall never consent.

B. In a few months more your consent will not be necessary.

Mrs. M. That brazen girl! I'll be revenged on her.

B. She is innocent in the matter. Save your spite for me.

Mrs. M. Ky. Brantford, beware. I still have influence; I'll expose your knavery.

B. Mrs. Milford, when you speak of your influence and my knavery it would be well to remember that you profited by that knavery, also that I hold a mortgage on all you possess, and that your extravagance has placed the means of payment beyond your reach. What have you to say about Hopper's part in the affair?

Mrs. M. I shall learn all the facts from him.

B. (*Bowing coldly.*) Thanks, Madam, for the confidence you repose in *my* statement. If a month's wages is due him, perhaps you would do well to pay it. He may need the money for traveling expenses.

Mrs. M. Do you presume to discharge my people?

B. Oh, I only suggest. If you don't get rid of him, I can, that's all!

Mrs. M. Oh, Mr. Brantford, please don't drive him from the country!

B. (*With a sneer.*) So you know my power at last!

Mrs. M. Please, for my sake, don't harm him!

B. Well, I'll not harm him. We will give him and that nigger just twenty-four hours to leave the country. They are already on the black list.

Mrs. M. (*Bursts into tears.*) Oh, this is too much! Mr. Brantford, I beg you will leave my house at once.

B. Pray, Madam, don't excite yourself. No harm will come of it. I will see you when you are more collected. Good day. (*Exit L.*)

Mrs. M. (*Sinks in chair, C.*) Oh, the despicable wretch! To think that I ever cared for such a monster! Thank heaven I know him now, but, alas, it may be too late. He trifled with my feelings while he robbed me, and to think of preferring Rose, a mere servant. Oh, the shame! But I may punish his impertinence yet. (*Exit, R.*)

CURTAIN

ACT V.

SCENE.—*Mrs. Milford's. A few months elapse between acts IV and V.*

B. (Pacing floor.) Once I was not obliged to wait for an audience with the charming widow. I was a trifle more popular with her then than now. But then we talked more agreeable subjects, now we talk business entirely. The mortgage is due to-day, and the proceedings for foreclosure will need but little time.

Enter MRS. MILFORD, *L.*

(Bowing formally.) Ah, good day, Mrs. Milford, I trust you are quite well.

Mrs. M. (Coldly.) I am well. I presume you called on business?

B. I did!

Mrs. M. Take a seat. *(They take seats, R and L of table.)* I have no money.

B. Ten thousand dollars is a large sum.

Mrs. M. It is customary to give a little extension of time, is it not?

B. That is at the option of the mortagee. I informed you in my note of my decision. The money must be paid.

Mrs. M. Brantford, you are a hard man.

B. Spare your epithets, Madam. Will you pay?

Mrs. M. I am unable to do so. This is a gross injustice! You know that I never received the worth of my money on these so-called improvements. I think the contractor and yourself could explain why.

B. Mrs. Milford, this is a waste of words. When the proceedings were begun to set aside your late husband's will, I think you had good reason to suspect that some things about the case were crooked. That decision put much money into your pocket. You kept silent then.

Mrs. M. It is false! I supposed everything was done legitimately.

B. Then you know very little of business.

Mrs. M. That I have learned to my sorrow.

B. There is one way to settle this difficulty which may prove satisfactory.

Mrs. M. What is that?

B. If Rose will become my wife, she remains here as mistress of this house. I will allow her to make a *reasonable* provision for you.

Mrs. M. Enough of that! When did this all happen?

B. You can at least communicate my wishes to her.

Mrs. M. You would humiliate me.

B. Not at all. It's very natural to ask the mother to inter-cede with the daughter.

Mrs. M. I will try. (*Exit, R.*)

B. I fancy these headstrong women at last begin to listen to reason. Really it is too bad to be compelled to use such convinc-ing arguments but Kyle Brantford never failed yet. This time I rather think the young lady will change her tune a little as the mother has already done.

Enter ROSE, *R.*

R. Speak! I am prepared!

B. Oh! I see! Doubtless you are aware of the purport of what I am about to say. Your mother is unable to meet her obliga-tions. Unless a means of settlement is found the family will be homeless and penniless to-morrow. That would really be very unpleasant. If you are willing to become my wife I will make some provision for Mrs. Milford and you shall be mistress here.

R. Mr. Brantford, I have already told you twice that I do not love you, that I never can love you. Would you wish a wife whose life would be one ever present lie? My heart is already another's.

B. And that other will never return to claim it. Why does he not write you and fulfill his promise? Doubtless you will learn in time to love me. Remember much depends on your decision. In half an hour the sheriff of the county will be here to post a notification of sale on the door. Perhaps a brief reflec-tion would assist you in reaching a final decision. I will saunter in the cool breeze while you consider the matter. (*Exit, L.*)

R. (*Sinks into a chair, C.*) The fates seem determined to plunge me into this awful pit. What *shall* I do to save myself from a fate infinitely worse than death? Am I deceived in every-body? Frank has never sent me a single line though I know he is well and prosperous. Brantford is successful in everything. First Frank and then Hopper and Zeke were obliged to flee the county. Mother was flattered, deceived; and is now a beggar with no power to help me if she would. Polly is my only friend. Brantford speaks fair. May be 'tis as well, though death were preferable.

Enter POLLY, *suddenly, R.*

P. (*With joyous manner.*) Rose, I've ever such good news!

R. What is it, Polly?

P. I've heard from the boys, and Ike is here!

R. Here!

P. Yes, don't speak so loud. You see I knew there was something wrong or Frank would write. So I wrote to Ike and told him all about it and got him to ask Frank to write to you again

R. You shouldn't have done that, Polly.
P. Shouldn't I though! Just read that! (*Hands Rose a note.*)
R. (*Reads.*)

DEAR ROSE.—I have written you several times since I left home but have never received any letters. I concluded that you wished to forget me. But I learn through Mr. Hopper, that there is a great mistake somewhere. Remember our parting pledge. I agreed to rescue you in case of danger. I have learned many things from Cliffville, and I know you are in danger. Will you meet me at the big spring at seven?

Yours ever,
FRANK.

What would you do, Polly?
P. Go.
R. Yes, it is the only thing left.
P. Ike has come for you.
R. (*Surprised.*) Where is he?
P. In the kitchen. Sooky is calling on a neighbor but may be home any minute. Get ready! I'll bring Ike. (*Exit, R.*)
R. How sudden! It's too good to be true. I never could believe Frank false. (*Seizes her hat.*) But I haven't a moment to spare. (*Puts on hat.*)

Enter IKE *and* POLLY, *R.*

R. Ike, I'm so glad to see you. (*Seizes his hand.*)
I. No more than I am to see you, Miss Rose.
R. Polly, get my riding skirt, a thick shawl and a pair of overshoes. (*Exit Polly, L.*) Where is Frank?
I. Stoppin' at the the ten mile tavern, to-day. He's at the big spring by this time. We've good horses.
R. Hark! I hear footsteps. It is Sooky Button. We are lost! She is coming here. (*Ike pulls sofa from the wall suddenly and hides himself behind it.*)

Enter SOOKY, *R.*

S. Why! are you by yourself, Rose? I thought I heard talkin'.
R. Polly just went up stairs. (*Goes to the door L, and calls Polly.*) Polly, Miss Button wants you.
S. I didn't say I wanted her. Reckon she may come though and be gettin' the turns done. This room hasn't been red up to-day, I believe. Looks like it.
R. (*Hastily.*) Miss Button, don't you think that is a stain coming on the wall there? (*Points in a direction opposite to Ike.*)
S. Like enough. There's a desprit lot o' stains in the kitchen. (*Going, R.*) Send that gal in when she comes. (*Exit, R.*)
I. (*Crawls out.*) That was an awful close shave.
R. I was frightened nearly to death. (*In her excitement she drops Frank's note.*)

Enter POLLY.

P. Here are the things Rose, all in a bundle.
I. All ready?
R. Yes!
I. You go down the path by the orchard, I'll take the road. In three minutes we will defy the best horses in the county. Good bye, Polly!
P. Good bye! Be smart, an' mighty keerful! Good bye, Rose.
R. Farewell, Polly. (*Kisses her.*)
P. Take the side gate through the garden. (*Exeunt Rose and Ike, R.*) Well that's the excitin'est thing I ever did see. My heart's cuttin' up like an alarm clock. If they're found out and overtook I reckon we'll all ketch it.

Enter BRANTFORD, L.

B. Polly, where is Miss Milford? (*Polly hesitates.*) Why don't you answer, girl? Where is Miss Milford, I said.
P. (*Starts.*) Oh, I beg pardon, sir! I s'pect—I 'low—
B. Well, what do you 'spect?
P. That she is in her room.
B. Then why didn't you say so? Call her. (*Exeunt Polly, L.*) Now for the final answer. I think my lady understands the case by this time. We will have no more haggling. (*Sees note. Picks it up and reads.*) Why, what is this? "Meet me at the big spring at seven. Yours, Frank." An elopement, curse it! By heavens, I'll not be foiled. They can't be far yet. Where is that blockhead Button, that I hired for such emergencies! Drunk or asleep, I'll bet. (*Looks at his watch.*) Ten minutes before seven. They haven't gone far yet. I'll bring her back in spite of fate. (*Rushes out, L.*)

Enter POLLY, L.

P. There he goes, like a crazy man! and Rose isn't half across the orchard yet. It's no use tryin' any more, oh my—oh—

Enter MRS. M., L.

Mrs. M. Why are you so excited?
P. (*Excitedly.*) I'm afraid he'll kill Ike.
Mrs. M. Who threatens Isaac with danger? Something has happened. What is it? Speak, girl!
P. It's dreadful! Frank sent Ike back to get Rose an' they've eloped an' Ky. Brantford is after them.
Mrs. M. Girl, are you out of your senses?
P. No! But I think you were when you trusted Ky. Brantford.
Mrs. M. She has a strong will and I have little influence over her.

P. (Breathlessly.) Oh, it all happened this minnit an' I'm scart nearly to death. *(Bell rings.)*

Mrs. M. Go to the door, Polly. *(Exit Polly, L.)* What does this commotion all mean! Will troubles never cease?

Enter POLLY L, showing in sheriff.

Sheriff. Madam, I am the sheriff of Cliff County.

Mrs. M. I have expected you. Do your duty and advertise the place for sale. I am helpless.

Sheriff. Do not be alarmed, madam, unnecessarily. Just now my business is with Mr. Brantford.

Mrs. M. He was here a few moments ago and I am expecting him again.

Sheriff. Then I will take a turn on the lawn till he arrives. *(Exit, L.)*

Mrs. M. I cannot endure this suspense! *(Exit L.)*

P. I'm in a dreadful worked up perdicament. I'll just go up stairs and look if Rose is still in sight. *(Exit, R.)*

Enter ROSE and BRANTFORD, L.

B. (Ironically.) Your short walk has put a glow in your cheeks. Really it has improved your appearance very much.

R. (Indignantly.) Mr. Brantford, hitherto I have endured your insults in silence. But I will do so no longer. You have defrauded us of all we possessed, let that satisfy you. You have acted under semblance of law, but when you lay hands on me to detain me, you violate law! I will have you arrested for assault.

B. Humph! Better save your time and trouble! I know something of the law in *this* county. You were about to do a foolish thing and I prevented you. The judge will only say I was your benefactor and admonish you. Besides, when a young lady is caught attempting to elope the less she says about it the better. It doesn't look well, my dear!

R. Don't call me your dear! Brantford, leave this room!

Enter suddenly L., FRANK, SHERIFF, IKE, ZEKE, MRS. M., POLLY, BOB, and followed in a moment by SOOKY BUTTON.

F. The sooner the better! Coward, how dare you insult a helpless girl?

R. Oh, it is Frank! *(Rushes to his side.)*

F. Yes, dear Rose, I will protect you now.

B. I hardly expected, young man, that you would come to boast of your latest exploit! Are you sure you can protect yourself?

F. I have not come to boast but to claim my own and defend the rights of others as you shall presently see. *(Nods to the sheriff who steps to front, L. C., passing Ky.)*

B. Mr. Blake, have you notified Mrs. Milford of the sale of these premises?

Sheriff. I have not. Instead I have a paper which interests you. It is a warrant for your arrest on charge of conspiracy.

B. (*Starting back.*) My arrest! I'll never be taken! Stand back! (*Draws pistol.*)

Sheriff. Seize him, boys! (*Zeke and Hopper suddenly pinion Brantford and he is disarmed. If the company think proper this scene may be worked up a little and the pistol discharged.*)

B. You shall all rue this! You don't know me yet.

I. Keep cool, Mr. Brantford. There's no Regulators here but there are half a dozen Squir'l Hunters on the porch. (*Bob is seen slipping out.*)

Sheriff. Robert Button is an accomplice! Seize him!

I. (*Catching Bob.*) Robert, (*with comical expression*) the county judge wants you. The sheriff 'ill interduce yer, I reckon.

Bob. I haint done nothin'.

Sheriff. The less you talk the better for you

Mrs. M. What is the meaning of all this company, Mr. Blake?

Sheriff. The prisoners are charged with conspiring to defraud the heirs of the late Asa Milford. The proceedings in the settlement of the estate will all doubtless be set aside, thanks to the indefatigable efforts of Mr. Colewood.

S. Laws to goodness! brother Bob don't know the least mite about a conspiracy. He never seed one in his life. He is as innocent as a—

Z. A yalligator!

Sheriff. Come, Brantford and Button, we must go. Don't be downcast. There's plenty of company outside. (*Exeunt Sheriff and prisoners, L.*)

S. (*Following.*) You're all a pack of dirty scamps! If you hurt Bob I'll scald every one o' you. (*Exit, L.*)

F. (*Taking Rose's hand.*) Dear Rose, our anxieties shall soon end.

R. I cannot tell you how grateful and happy I am, and it is all so sudden.

Z. Dat pistol whopped out sort o' suddent.

F. The villains interrupted all my letters! but I toiled to collect evidence. I determined you should have your own. I feared to wait longer and determined on your rescue, and strangely enough the sheriff was ready just as we came.

R. How could I ever lose my faith in you? Forgive me! (*Ike and Polly whisper aside.*)

F. There is nothing to forgive.

Mrs. M. It is I who must ask your forgiveness. I weakly yielded to the promptings of vanity and avarice. I have done you both a great wrong. Children, can you forgive me? I, too, have suffered.

F. With all my heart!

R. I am too happy to refuse did I wish it, and I, too, forgive you, Mrs. Milford.

I. Polly, hadn't we better jine hands?

P. I think so, Ike.

Z. I golly, dere's only a vacancy for me.

I. You'll find somebody, Zeke, to fill the vacancy.

Mrs. M. (*To Frank and Rose.*) May heaven bless the union of two such loving hearts. (*To Frank.*) And may the devotion of the lover live in the affections of the husband.

F. (*Puts his hand around Rose's waist.*) Dear Rose, this shall fu fill the wishes of our father and benefactor as he breathed his last UNDER THE LAURELS.

DISPOSITION OF CHARACTERS.

L.	*C.*			*R.*
IKE AND POLLY.	FRANK.	ROSE.	MRS. M.	ZEKE:

NOTHING BETTER THAN THE SCRAP-BOOK RECITATION SERIES

BY H. M. SOPER.

PRICE, POST PAID, PAPER, 25 CENTS

"The selections are choice in quality and in large variety."—*Inter-Ocean*, Chicago.
"It excels anything we have seen for the purpose."—*Eclectic Teacher*.
"The latest and best things from our popular writers appear here."—*Normal Teacher*

CONTENTS OF NO. 1.

T. S. DENISON, Publisher,

163 Randolph St., - - CHICAGO.

ETHIOPIAN PLAYS.

Price 15 Cents Each, Postpaid.

These plays are all short, and very funny. Little or no stage apparatus is required. The number of darkies is given in those plays in which white characters occur.

STAGE STRUCK DARKEY.

A very funny burlesque on high acting; 2 m., 1 f. Time, 10 m. Three negroes play Claude Melnotte, Lady Macbeth, Macduff, "Lucimicus," Damon and Pythias, etc.

STOCKS UP—STOCKS DOWN.

2 m. A played-out author and his sympathizing friend. Time, 8 m. Very funny and full of business. Ludicrous description of a fire.

DEAF—IN A HORN.

2 m. Negro musician and a deaf pupil. Time, 8 m. The "pupil" has a large horn which he uses for an ear trumpet, pretending to be very deaf. By stratagem the teacher causes him to hear suddenly.

HANDY ANDY.

2 m., master and servant. Time, 12 m. Servant makes all sorts of ludicrous mistakes, and misunderstands every order.

THE MISCHIEVOUS NIGGER.

A very popular farce; 4 m., 2 f. Time, 20 m. (Only one darky, the mischievous nigger.) Scene: Chamber and bedroom off. Requires two sham babies. Characters: Antony Snow (the nigger), old man, French barber, Irishman, nurse, Mrs. Norton.

THE SHAM DOCTOR.

A negro farce; 4 m., 2 f. Time, 15 m. Liverheel turns doctor, and practices on "old Johnson." The sham doctor will bring down the house.

NO CURE, NO PAY.

3 m. (1 darky), 1 f. Time, 10 m. Will suit the most fastidious; a good piece for school or parlor.

HAUNTED HOUSE.

2 m , landlord and a whitewasher (also 2 or 3 ghosts.) Time, 8 m. The whitewasher discovers spirits in a house where he is at work, and is frightened badly in consequence.

AN UNHAPPY PAIR.

3 m. (and males for a band.) Time, 10 m. Two hungry "niggers" strike the musicians for a square meal. Good for school or parlor. Very funny; ends with a burlesque duet.

THE TWO POMPEYS.

4 m. Time, 8 m. A challenge to a duel is worked up in a very humorous manner until the courage oozes out of the duellists.

TRICKS.

A negro farce; 5 m., 2 f. Time, 10 m. (Only 2 darkies, 1 m., 1 f.)

THE JOKE ON SQUINIM.

A negro farce (Black Statue improved), by W. B. Sheddaw; 4 m., 2 f. Time, 25 m. Scenes: A barn and a plain room.

QUARRELSOME SERVANTS.

3 m. Time, 8 m. Mr. Jenkins is unable to procure servants who will not quarrel. He advertises for a male cook and an hostler. The interview with the candidates is uproariously comical.

SPORTS ON A LARK.

3 m. Time, 8 m. Two niggers who are dead broke meet and get acquainted. Business is very lively and taking.

OTHELLO AND DESDEMONA.

2 m. Time, 12 m. A side-splitting burlesque on Othello. The strangling of "Desdemona" will bring down the house every time.

BACK FROM CALIFORNY; Or, Old Clothes.

3 m. Time, 12 m. Things get badly mixed and the clothes are locked in the wrong trunks.

UNCLE JEFF.

A farce. 5 m. (2 negroes,) 2 f. Time, 25 m. A very popular farce.

ALL EXPENSES; Or Nobody's Son.

2 m. Time, 10 m. Artemus Buz is a manager, and Jemius Fluticus applies for a situation in his company. Very funny.

PROF. BLACK'S FUNNYGRAPH.

A nigger burlesque on the phonograph; 6 m., and niggers for audience (on the stage). Time, 15 m.

JUMBO JUM.

A farce. 4 m. (1 negro), 3 f. Time, 30 m. A popular farce wherever negro humor of the stage type is appreciated.

T. S. DENISON, Publisher, 163 Randolph Street, CHICAGO.

www.ingramcontent.com/pod-product-compliance
Lightning Source LLC
Chambersburg PA
CBHW030907260626
47169CB00008B/2725